Willit the Amazing Wombat

A story in two parts by Frances Maber

Illustrated by Alexander Hills

Family Life & The Great Rescue

This book is for William,
who supported and encouraged the development of a "bee in my bonnet" until it became three books:
Willit's Friends, Willit the Wombat Grows Up and *Willit the Amazing Wombat.*

Author's Note:

Willit is a Northern Hairy-nosed Wombat. Apart from the characters in this book, all his relatives live in Epping Forest in central Queensland. There are not very many of them and they need help if they are to be like Willit and raise families. Just buying this book is a way of assisting them.

Wombats are amazing creatures. They do all of the things that you will find in this book – except that when they communicate they use their own language. Their greeting sounds like "Huh."

Could a wombat manage a 'great rescue'? Maybe. You can make up your own mind.

The other creatures in the book are found all over Australia, though in some places different names may be used.

Illustrator's Note: Alexander E Hill

When Frances first approached me about Willit illustrations, I must admit I felt rather ignorant about wombats. I had been producing posters for the Albany Classic Auto Event, painting watercolours and oils for exhibition for the last 40 years or so and the only animals I had been commissioned to draw were horses, cats and dogs and the occasional elephant. I had never seen a wombat. Never held a wombat. What did a Hairy-nosed Wombat look like? I really had no idea that there were different types of wombat.

Frances told me that wombats, especially the Northern Hairy-nosed sort, are in danger of becoming extinct. I would not like that to happen and neither would Willit. If my illustrations could help him and his family in their quest for survival, then I would try very hard to learn how to draw them. The next step is to say "Hello" to a real wombat one day.

Family Life

It was a warm night. The full moon flooded the bush with light and turned the pond gold. It lit up Willit's front door but he wasn't there. It sent a beam along his track up the rocky cliff but he wasn't there either. It peeped down through the branches of a large banksia tree and found him.

Willit left his burrow by its secret back door. He sniffed the night air. Pollen from the wattle flowers tickled his nose and he sneezed loudly. The moon shone on his favourite path. It beckoned him to come adventuring. He was soon deep in the bush.

As he jogged along he practised his marching song. He couldn't sing, of course, but he liked to pretend.

I'm a wombat, I live in the bush,
If something's in my way I give it a push.
I'm like a bull-dozer on four short legs
And I only eat greens, never meat or eggs.

Willit stopped. He was under a huge gum tree that hid the moon. He looked around and found it again. He sniffed. A soft wombat smell floated on the air.

"I'll investigate," he thought. "Perhaps it's a new friend." He left the shadows and followed the moon.

Strong and brave and I live underground,
In burrow that I dig, with claws tough and round.
I eat in the night and I sleep by day
Then I visit my friends if I want to play.

Willit bulldozed his way through some thick bushes into a grassy patch. He saw another wombat. She looked at him. Neither of them said a word. They nibbled the grass. As they ate, they moved closer and closer until they bumped noses.

They went on eating but in between bites Willit looked at the stranger. She was very pretty. Willit wanted to talk to her but he had to think of something to say. At last he found his voice.

"Huh. Huh. Huh. Who are you?"

"A wombat, of course."

"Yes, but what's your name?"

"Just Wombat. Isn't that your name too?"

"No, I'm Willit. Willit the Wombat.
My Mum gave me a special name.
Didn't you get a special name
when you were little?"

"No. I've never met a wombat
with a special name."

"Can I give you one?"

"Yes, if you want to. What would it be?"

"I'll have to think. Let's walk for a bit."

Willit wanted to stop talking. Having 'a think' was a good way to do that. They sauntered off into the bush together, stopping now and again to feed. "Where do you live?" asked Willit.

"Back near where we met." His new friend stopped, shuddered then looked over her shoulder.

"What's wrong?"

"Dingoes. Don't you hear them?"

"Yes, but I don't care. Would you like to see my burrow? We're nearly there."

"Mmmm. Perhaps."

They walked on again till Willit suddenly said, "I think you're the prettiest wombat I've ever seen. My Aunt Sis is pretty and I know that my Mum was prettier than her but you're the prettiest of all. I've a name for you. It's Lady."

Lady dropped her head. She looked at her toes and she looked at Willit's toes. She swung her shoulders a bit and looked at her toes some more. "I'd like to be called Lady," she whispered. "I think you must be a special wombat to think of such a lovely name for me."

They stopped talking and Willit walked on until he came to his back door.

"Come and see my burrow," he said.

"Okay."

They entered the secret tunnel and made their way down, down, down to the main living chamber of Willit's home. Willit showed Lady the sleeping places and she chose one. It was nearly morning and they were tired. They both slept.

When they awoke, Willit told Lady about his aunt. Lady told Willit that her little brother had been taken by a dingo. "That's why you were frightened when you heard them howl," he said.

"Yes. I hate them."

"Don't worry. I'll look after you."

"Could you fight a dingo?"

"I'd try."

"How?"

"I'd back into him and he'd try biting my rump. Then I'd push him back into a tree or rock, heave my backside up and bang his head. That'd make him give in."

"Have you ever done that?"

"No, but the Great Wombat killed one dingo that way and another at his burrow's entrance."

"You're brave Willit."

"Not really but I am hungry. Do you like to eat newly grown reeds and rushes?"

"They're my favourite food."

"Follow me."

Willit led Lady through his front door to the pond and showed her how to paddle across its shallowest part. Once they were on the other side he went down-stream to a beautiful red-flowering gum tree then turned into the reed beds where the newest shoots grew. They had a feed before Willit walked to the gum tree and butted his head on the trunk.

"Whatever are you doing?"

Willit didn't answer. Instead, he sat on his haunches and looked up at the tree.

"Willit, Willit, Willit," called a cheery voice.

"We'll be with you in a minute."

Lady's eyes opened wide when two wagtails, one with a damaged wing, flew down and landed on Willit's back.

"Look at this, Lady," called Willit. "These are my special friends. They're called Willie and Wig-Wag."

Then he said to the birds: "This is Lady. She's my mate."

Willie jumped onto Lady's head. "I'm so glad you've met Willit," she whispered.

"He's very brave. A few days ago he saved Wig-Wag from a snake."

Lady stared. She rarely talked to birds. News of the snake adventure was a surprise.

She suspected that Willit was no ordinary wombat.

Wig-Wag needed flying practice. Calling "See ya' later, see ya' later, see ya' later," the birds departed.

Lady and Willit stayed together for a few days. Every night they explored the bush near the pond. Sometimes they played chasey. Lady ran in a circle or a figure-of-eight and Willit followed until he caught her and rolled her over. During the day they slept or chatted inside Willit's burrow. They didn't know that CarS, the carpet snake, often watched them.

One evening, after a game of chasey, Lady decided to return to her own burrow. "I won't be coming home with you tonight, Willit," she said. This was unexpected but Willit didn't mind. He enjoyed Lady's company but he was happy on his own. "Will you tell me where your burrow is so that I can visit you?"

"Not now. I'll tell you next time we meet." Lady waddled away.

Neither of them knew that CarS followed her. He wanted to know where she lived.

"Oom, oom, gloom and doom," murmured Mr Frogmouth.

"Mopoke, Mopoke," croaked another dismal voice. "She's gone. I knew she would. Poor Willit's alone again."

Wombats never laugh but when Willit heard the birds he almost chuckled. "I'm not alone," he shouted. "I'm the happiest wombat in the bush. Lady is my mate. We'll meet again when she's ready." Then he did a 'wombat special' – twice! He pounced onto his front feet, shot a back leg out behind then curled it up over his back till he tickled his ears. It felt so good that he did it again with the other leg. He tried to do it with both legs at once but that didn't quite work. It needed practice!

Lurking in a hollow log Mr Chuditch saw this amazing sight. It made him jealous. No matter how he tried he could not imitate the lumbering great wombat! High in the tree-tops Pinky-Grey the galah woke up and saw it too. Next day she told the flock and the bush rang with reports that Willit had been doing the 'wombat special'. He was very happy.

Willit's life resumed its old rhythm. His burrow was the centre of his range. From it, he went on long marches in all directions, adding more words to his song as he went.

I've a tough plate hidden in my rump,

I haven't got much tail, just that bony lump

And it is all covered with skin so thick,

That it keeps me quite safe from a bite or kick.

Every evening, from a sitting place near his front door, Willit watched Willie and Wig-Wag. The birds built a nest where Willie laid three eggs. When they hatched, she named the babies One, Two and Three. They all learned to ride on Willit's back. CarS thought about attacking the birds but many friends guarded them. Instead, he often travelled through the bush to watch what was happening at Lady's burrow.

Once or twice Willit wondered if he should look for Lady but he was content to wait until she reappeared. He forgot about CarS. He listened for Dingo and was glad that he never heard his howl.

Summer passed and autumn arrived. Early one morning, Willit paused at the top of the rocky cliff to look down at his front door. It was still a bit dark but he could see another wombat on the sand. As he trundled down the path, a voice he knew called "Hello Willit."

"Lady, you've come to visit me. Will you come into the burrow?"
"Yes please," she said. "I'm tired. It's a long walk from my burrow to yours."

As soon as she was underground, Lady shook her back leg. Out of her pouch tumbled a very small wombat. It walked round and stood by Lady's front legs.
"You've got a joey. You *are* clever Lady."
"I think we're both clever! Our son arrived on the night of the great storm so I called him Thunder."

She gave another shake. Out of her pouch tumbled another baby. It stood beside Thunder. It was smaller than him.
"Two joeys! I've never heard of that before."
"It's great, isn't it!" said Lady. "My mum said that it's *very special* to have twins. As soon as our daughter crawled into my pouch I knew that something wonderful had happened. That's why I called her Wonder."
Lady looked at her babies. "Now you two, say hello to Willit. He's your Papa."
"Hello Willit," said two very small voices.

Baby wombats were a new experience for Willit. He flopped onto his tummy to have a good look.

"You're beautiful," he told them. "Will you all live in my burrow now, Lady?"

"No, Willit. They're so small that with two of us trundling in and out, we could easily hurt them. I'll go back to my own burrow but you can come and visit. Would you baby-sit now? I'd like a nap."

Lady went up one of the side tunnels to a sleeping chamber leaving the twins with Willit.

For a while nothing was said as four tiny eyes looked into two big ones.

"It must be crowded in the pouch when you're both in there," remarked Willit.

"Yes Papa, it is," replied Thunder. "Mumma says we wriggle so much that our claws dig into her side. Did you wriggle in the pouch when you were small?"

"Yes, I did. If I wriggled too much my mum'd say "Ouch". Then she'd shake her pouch and tell me to sit still."

"That's just what Mumma does," said Wonder.

"She never lets us out when we're in the bush Not even if it's really hot," moaned Thunder.

"What do you do?" asked Willit.

The twins nudged each other.

"Thunder has a trick," said Wonder. "He rides with his feet hanging out of the pouch. I have a turn too. It's fun!"

Willit wasn't sure this was proper behaviour so he said nothing. Wonder wriggled a bit and for the first time Willit looked at the top of her head. He asked her to sit very still while he checked the fur behind her ears.

When Lady returned she found the twins curled up asleep between Willit's paws. Willit was watching them with his nose resting gently on his daughter's back.
"Come and look," he whispered. "Our Wonder is just like my mother. She has white hairs behind both her ears."
Lady looked at Wonder's head. "I was surprised when I saw those white hairs. I've never seen fur that colour before. We're lucky wombats."
"No doubt about that," said Willit.

It was time for a proper sleep. Lady woke the twins and tucked them into her pouch. They needed to be there for warmth and food. Once they were packed in she went to a sleeping chamber.
Willit didn't. He slept with his rump in the end of the main tunnel. He didn't want any strangers wandering into his burrow.

Late in the afternoon the wombats woke up. The twins explored the main part of the burrow until Lady said it was time to go. She told them to get into her pouch but Willit had a different idea. He went outside for a minute to test the temperature. It was still warm.

"It must be hard work having two in the pouch, Lady."

"It is. Carrying them both around makes me tired."

"What about having Wonder in the pouch and letting me carry Thunder on my back. His fur is thicker than his sister's and it's still warm outside."

"Yes please Mumma, let me do that," shouted Thunder.

"I'd like to have the pouch to myself," said Wonder, as she scrambled into the rumble seat.

"I'm not sure about this," murmured Lady. "Thunder isn't a bird, you know."

"I know," replied Willit, "but let's try." He led the way out of the burrow then lay on the ground.

"Climb onto my back, Thunder, and dig your front claws into the fur on my neck. Spread your back legs so that your tummy is right down in my fur. Are you ready?"

"Yes, Papa, I think so." Thunder was a bit scared but he didn't show it. Just then Willie flew across the pond.

"Willit, Willit, Willit, Lady, Lady, Lady," she chirped "What's this I see? A baby wombat in my place on Willit's back! This is good news."

"There's more good news than just one joey," said Willit proudly. "Look at Lady's rumble seat." The bird walked behind Lady and there, peeping out between her Mumma's back legs, was Wonder.

"Oh you clever things. You have twins. I'll fly off and tell everyone in the bush. Goodbye, goodbye, goodbye," she chanted. She told Wig-Wag first and before the wombats had climbed the track up the rocky cliff, she'd gone in one direction and her mate in the other to spread the news about Willit's family.

Willit and Lady trotted non-stop, all the way to Lady's burrow. Willit put Thunder down on the ground then sniffed around the entrance. "Don't go in there, Lady," he warned. "You've got a visitor."
"Thunder! Into my pouch! Quickly!" Lady turned to Willit. "What is it?"
"I think it's that wicked carpet snake," he replied.
"Yesss," hissed an unpleasant voice. "Yesss. It'sss me. Now clear off. Thisss burrow sssuitsss me for my winter sssleep."
Lady was horrified. "Come away, Willit. I can't bear snakes. We'll go back to your burrow."
Willit knew that was the only thing to do. He couldn't fight CarS while the snake was underground.

It was an *awful* journey back to the pond. It was cold and the twins had to be in Lady's pouch. They were frightened. Lady was tired. Dingoes howled in the distance. At last they reached the banksia tree and Willit sent his family into his burrow while he stayed above ground.

First he filled in the secret entrance to his home then he had a quick feed before going down the cliff to his front door. Once inside he blocked the main tunnel with his body. He didn't sleep. He stayed on guard.

Next evening Willit went back alone to see what he could do about CarS. He was surprised to find the entrance to Lady's burrow covered by a beautiful web. One of his black spider friends sat in the middle of it.

"Hi Willit," said the spider.

Willit stared. "Hello," he said. "Aren't you worried that CarS will come out and break your web?"

"The snake has gone. I've been waiting here to see you."

"How do you know he's gone?"

"When CarS stole Lady's burrow, I asked my family if we could get him out. We talked to our distant cousins, the Red Backs."

"You mean the poisonous clan?"

"That's right. They agreed to help."

"How could they?"

"Hush and I'll tell you. Early this morning Widow Red Back, the most poisonous of all, arrived and marched into the burrow. CarS was asleep so she took up her position on his nose. CarS opened an eye and got an awful fright. Widow Red Back told him that she wanted the burrow and that she'd bite him on the mouth if he didn't leave immediately."

"What did CarS do?"

"He moved out fast. Magpie followed him to the hollow log he uses when he sleeps. He'll be there for ages."

"Wow!" said Willit. He thought a bit. "Where's Widow Red Back now?"

"Don't worry about her! She's gone back to her favourite tree stump. Lady's burrow is empty."

"Thank you, Black Spider. Thank Widow Red Back too."

"I will." Black Spider moved as Willit broke the delicate web and entered Lady's burrow. He dug out all traces of the snake before hurrying back to the pond.

Willit loved having a family. Often he helped Lady look after Thunder and Wonder. Mostly, Lady and the twins slept in her burrow but sometimes she brought them to stay with their Papa. The bush folk got used to the sight of the adults walking together, one of the twins riding on Willit's back and the other peeping out of Lady's rumble seat. Whenever they were near the pond the Wagtail Family joined them on their rambles.

By the time the twins were ten months old they were able to eat bush tucker. They no longer rode in the pouch so one day Willit surprised them all.

"Let's have a holiday," he said.

"Yes please Papa," yelled the twins.

"Where shall we go?" asked Lady.

"We'll walk back to the Old Burrow and visit my aunt."

"What a great idea," said Lady, so they went.

Aunt Sis was very pleased to see them. Willit's family was the first from that part of the bush to have twins. All the wombats that lived there came to see them - all except the Great Wombat. He was away on a journey. When he returned, he heard that Willit had grown again and that he had a mate and two joeys.

Everyone knew that now Willit was the biggest, strongest wombat in the bush.

The Great Rescue

The holiday was over so Willit and his family said goodbye to
Aunt Sis and their friends.

"Will you use the same track to get back to the pond?" asked Aunt Sis.

"No. I've decided on a new route. We'll cut through the bush and arrive
home in two nights."

"Come and visit us again. The Great Wombat will be sorry to have
missed you."

They set off, Willit leading, followed by Thunder and Wonder. Lady came last.
She liked to keep an eye on her twins. Their chattering was the only sound heard.

"Hey Wonder. Wasn't it funny how everyone thought us younger than we are?"

"Yep. They seemed to think we're only just out of the pouch. Why was that,
Mumma?"

"It's because you're twins," said Lady. "With two in the pouch you're a bit smaller
than one joey would be. You're growing quickly. You'll soon catch up."

"Did you like that jumping-down game they taught us?" Thunder asked his sister.

"Ooh yes! It's fun to be up high and then jump down. I want to keep practising that."

"You're good at it," said her brother. "I enjoyed the jumping-across game most."

"Of course," said Wonder, "because you jumped over wider spaces than any of the others."

"You're both good at jumping," said Lady. "I think I'll call you my Jumperoos!"

"Papa, did you hear that? Mumma's got a new name for us."

Willit grunted. He was busy bulldozing a track through thick scrub. He had no energy for conversation.

Just before sunrise, they stopped for breakfast and to camp for the day. Willit and Lady began digging a burrow while their joeys played in the bush.

"Don't go far," warned Lady. "Make sure you can always hear us digging."

"Okay Mumma," chorused the twins, as they wandered off to practise being Jumperoos.

Each time Wonder scrambled onto a log, she jumped down the other side. Each time Thunder jumped across sunbeams or broken branches he moved forward.

They forgot to listen for the sound of their parents digging.

"Look at this big log. I'd like to jump off it," said Wonder.

"I'll help you up," said her brother. As Wonder used her front claws to climb the log, Thunder shoved from behind. It wasn't easy but she got to the top, balanced carefully and looked down the other side.

"Ooh, it's a bit high," she murmured. "I'll have to be careful where I land."

Thunder checked the ground. "What about that spot with lots of leaves?" he suggested.

"Looks good," Wonder said. "It'll be soft to land on. Watch me jump."

CRASH!

Wonder landed on the leaves but everything went wrong.
The leaves opened and she fell into a deep hole with shiny tin
sides. It was a trap.
"Help! Help!" she cried, as she landed with a thump at the
bottom of the pit.

Thunder crept through the leaves to the top of the hole. It was
dark down there but he could just see the top of his sister's head. "Are you all right?" he called.
"Yes, but my foot hurts and so does my nose. I can't get out. What'll we do?" she wailed.
"Dunno."
"I think you must get Papa."
"Yep, I won't be long. Don't go away."
Wonder snorted. "Not funny!" she said.

Thunder set off to find his parents. They were further away than he thought. It took him ages to
reach them.

Wonder cowered at the bottom of the hole. In her fright she began to hiccough. She heard wings
swooshing above the hole. Looking up she saw a very bright eye looking down at her.

"You're in a pickle," said the bird.

"I'm not in a pickle, I'm in a hole," said Wonder.

The bird lifted her head, spread her hackles and gargled with delight.

"You're not scared, I can tell that. It's good to know you're made of tough stuff."

"Course I am. I've got special parents called Willit and Lady. I'm Wonder and my twin brother, Thunder, is fetching Papa."

"I've heard of your family. I'm pleased to meet you."

"You're a raven aren't you?"

"Yes. How did you know?"

"Because Mumma taught Thunder and me that only ravens make an argle-gargle."

"You have a clever Mumma. Tell you what, little one, I'll keep you company till your Papa arrives."

"Thanks," said Wonder. "Ooww!" she yelled.

"What's wrong?"

"I just put my foot down. It hurts. So does my nose. Mumma will be cross with me." Wonder began to hiccough again. Above the hole, Raven cocked her head. "Little one, I hear footsteps. People are coming. I won't go away. I'll perch in a tree. Be very quiet." Raven flew to a tree and watched.

Into the clearing strode two people. "Three cheers," said the man. "We've caught something in the pit trap. Hope it's that wretched cat that's been killing baby birds." He took a torch out of his pocket and shone it down the hole.

Wonder was terrified. The torch beam felt as if the sun was shining straight into her eyes. She dropped her head and tried to be invisible.

"Jenny, look at this. It's a baby wombat."
"What? How on earth did it get there?"
"Where's the long handled grabber?"
Jenny passed the grabber, took the torch and watched as Sid put the grabber down the hole and moved it until he had it round the joey's tummy. Very gently, he lifted Wonder out of the hole and put her into Jenny's arms. "She's a beauty," she said. "She's not very old. How did she get here? Why didn't her parents dig her out of our trap?" As she talked, Jenny examined Wonder. When she squeezed her front leg, Wonder pulled it away.
"She's got a cut nose and an injured front left foot. I think we'd better take her to the Sanctuary. She must be an orphan. Put her in the carry box, Sid, and we'll take her now."

Jenny and Sid left the clearing. They didn't seem to notice that Raven watched everything they did and flew after them. From her box, Wonder saw the bird. She felt safe because Raven was there.

Jenny and Sid found their quad bike and while Sid drove, Jenny sat on the back with Wonder's box on her knee. Raven had no trouble keeping them in sight. She followed just above the tree tops.

They left the bush for a road, followed it then entered a pair of tall wire gates. Sid parked their bike and he and Jenny took Wonder into a building. Raven perched in a tree. She must know what happened to Wonder before looking for Willit and Lady.

In the bush there was great unhappiness. Thunder had run as fast as he could back to his parents. They were shocked when he arrived alone. "Where's Wonder?" they asked. Puffing and panting, Thunder told his story.
"Come Lady," said Willit, "we must go at once. We'll have to dig Wonder out of that hole."

Thunder led his parents through the bush to the large tree trunk. He called out,
"Papa's here, Wonder. You'll soon be free." There was no reply. The three wombats crept to the hole and looked down. Wonder had gone.

"Ugh," said Lady, "there's a strange smell all around this hole. Something has taken Wonder and I don't know what it is. It smells different from any animal I've ever met."

The wombats huddled together in the shelter of the great tree trunk. Thunder was exhausted and fell asleep. His parents were too worried to sleep. They needed help but they didn't know where to look for it.

The sun was high in the sky before help came. "Rark, Rark. Wake up Willit. Wake up Willit. Rark, Rark," Raven called, as she skimmed over the trees. Willit heard. He shuddered. "Oh Lady, it's a raven. I haven't spoken to one since my mother was killed on the black track. This one wants to talk to me. I'm sure it's bad news."

He trundled out into the open, looked up and called: "I'm Willit."

Raven swooped down onto the tree trunk.

"I have good news," she called. "Wonder is safe and well. I can show you where she is."

"Why didn't you lead her back to us?"

"Because she's in a cage."

"What's a cage?" asked Lady.

"It's a place she can't leave. She's in the Sanctuary for animals that are hurt."

"But you said she was well," said Willit.

"Yes, she is. She has a little scratch on her nose and a sore front leg. She knows that I've come to find you. She trusts me."

Willit and Lady were surprised. Neither of them was inclined to trust Raven.

"How can we reach her?" asked Willit.

"When you get to the Sanctuary you'll need a messenger. A small bird is best. When I talked to Wonder I was chased away. Do you know a small bird that could help?"

"Yes," said Willit, "our friends the wagtails. They live in the red-flowering gum by the pond. Willie is sitting on eggs at the moment. Ask her children, One, Two and Three to come."

"Okay. I'll find them. You must walk in a straight line in that direction. There's a big grass tree with a tall flower spike way, way ahead on the top of a hill. When you arrive there, another friend will show you where to go next. Don't waste time."

With a sweep of her great wings, Raven departed.

26

"Come Lady, we must go at once." Willit set off at a swift jog. Lady followed. Thunder wasn't far behind, but he couldn't keep up.

"It's no good, Willit," called Lady. "I'll have to stop. The pace is too much for Thunder. He's not used to travelling in sunlight. He needs food and a proper sleep."

Willit paused. "You're right," he said. "I'll go on. You follow my track. We'll meet later." He left before Lady could say goodbye.

Willit came to a lake, ran in and swam straight across to the other shore.

He trotted up a hill. He arrived at a huge grass tree with a tall flower and looked for his guide. He couldn't see any of his friends. He sat on his haunches shouting,
"I'm here. Who'll help me find Wonder?"

The flower spike shook as a honey possum ran down it. "I'm here, Willit. Stand still and I'll jump onto your back." When the tiny possum was settled, he tweaked Willit's ears until the wombat was looking along the top of the ridge. "See the big gum tree way off in the distance?"
"Yes."

27

"That's where you have to go. Before you get there we'll pass some banksia trees and I'll leave you. There'll be another helper for you at the gum tree."

Willit started off again. He left the honey possum at the banksias and went on to the huge tree at the end of the ridge. Resting in its shade lay Mrs Wallaby with her joey by her side.

"Hello Willit," she said. "I'm your next guide."

"Okay," said Willit, "let's go."

"Not yet," she replied. "Sit down a minute. I want to tell you about the Sanctuary."

"How do *you* know about it?"

"Because that's where I grew up." Willit was so surprised that he sat down with a thump.

"When I was a joey," she began, "my mother was killed on the black track."

"Just like mine," cried Willit.

"That's right. I didn't know what to do. A strange creature arrived. It walked on its back legs and picked me up with its front legs. It put me in a bag a bit like my mother's pouch. When I got out of the bag I was in a cage with some other joeys. I lived in that cage until I was grown up. The strange creatures brought me food and water every day. Those creatures are called people."

"I've heard of people," muttered Willit. "The Great Wombat told me about them."

"There's a lot of them about," said Mrs Wallaby. "Some of them aren't very kind, but most of them are. At the Sanctuary they're all kind. Wonder will be safe with them. When I grew up, two people brought me and the other joeys back to the bush and set us free. Now, we must go." Mrs Wallaby stood up, tucked her joey into her pouch and led the way through the bush.

She stopped at last. "On the other side of that prickly scrub is a road."
"What's a road?"
"It's what you call a black track. We're not going on it but I want you to push through the scrub and look across to the other side. You'll see a thing that looks like a huge spider's web. It's called a wire fence. On the other side of the fence is the Sanctuary."

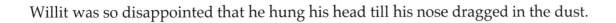

Willit followed Mrs Wallaby's instructions. He saw the black track. He looked across it and saw the huge thing like a web. He didn't see Wonder. He backed out of the scrub. "Where's my Wonder?" he asked.
"I can't help you with that but Raven will. I must take my joey back to the safety of the bush. Goodbye Willit." Mrs Wallaby disappeared.

Willit was so disappointed that he hung his head till his nose dragged in the dust.

"Willit, Willit, Willit. We're here, we're here, we're here."

"Rark. Rark. Reporting for duty."
Raven swooshed down to the ground as One,
Two and Three landed on Willit's back.
"We've been talking to Wonder," said One.
"She's not frightened 'cause she knows you're
here," said Two.
"We're going to carry messages across the high
fence," said Three.
"You're good friends," said Willit, "but how can
I get inside that web thing and get Wonder out?"
"Rark, Rark. Rescue and risks go together."
"Risks don't matter. I must rescue Wonder."
"Right. You'll think of a way. Relax now till it's
dark. We'll meet later." Raven sped away.

"One, Two and Three please go back to Wonder and tell her that Lady and Thunder are coming. Tell
her we're planning to see her. Tell her we'll set her free."

The wagtails flew over the fence while Willit withdrew to a shady spot for a snooze. When the sun
dropped behind the hills he awoke and went looking for food. Raven and the three wagtails arrived.
"Well Willit, what is your rescue plan?" asked Raven.
"Tell me something. Mrs Wallaby said that the big web thing is a wire fence. I can see through it.
Why can't I see Wonder?"
"That's easy. Inside are other fences made of wood. Wonder's behind a wooden fence."

"Okay. I'll burrow under the wire fence first, then find Wonder. I'll bulldoze a hole in her wooden fence and she'll be free."

"Right," said Raven. "First of all you must cross the road then burrow under the wire fence. Are you ready?"

"Yes… I don't like roads."

"The wagtails will make sure there's nothing on it, then you run straight across. I'll meet you at the first fence."

One and Two flew in opposite directions along the road. They whistled to Three.

"All clear," Three chirruped.

Without hesitation, Willit left the safety of the scrub and raced to the wire fence.

Raven led him to a spot close to Wonder's cage. "Burrow here," she said.

"The wagtails and I must sleep now. You'll find another friend waiting above Wonder's cage.".

Willit started to dig. The wire fence went underground a long way.

He had to dig down, down, down until he reached its edge.

Then he had to tunnel under it and up the other side.

It took much longer than he expected. By the time he was inside the Sanctuary it was almost morning.

He stood still and sniffed. The strange smell that Lady had noticed near the pit trap was very strong. Mixed with it were familiar animal smells. When Willit scented Wonder, he sat on his haunches and called. "I'm here, Wonder. Where are you?"

"Here, Papa. Here I am."

"Keep calling and I'll find you."

"Yes Papa. Here I am."

Willit walked while Wonder called. They made a lot of noise. Finally, he found the wooden wall that hid Wonder. Using his front claws, he hauled himself upwards until he stood on his back legs. He peeked over the top and saw his daughter. Two other baby wombats watched from a wooden shelter at the back of the cage.

The sun was rising.

"Wee-leet-squeak-me. See-me-tree. Wee-leet," called a strange voice. It was high pitched and the bits of words came out like drops of water rolling off a wet leaf. The only part Willit understood was "See-me-tree." He looked up. Hanging just above his head, face downwards, was a flying fox. "Pee-ple-near. Wee-leet-go. Me-stay-Won-der. Me-squeak-Wee-leet-lat-er."

Willit heard strange noises. Wonder heard them too. "I think people are coming," she called. "Go Papa, and come back tonight. Tell Mumma I'm not frightened and I've got plenty to eat."

Wonder ran back into the wooden shelter while Willit dashed to his tunnel. He was soon outside. Flying Fox checked the road and squeaked

"Go-go-go." Willit rushed across and found Lady and Thunder waiting.

Back in the Sanctuary Sid and Jenny began work for the day.

"Did you hear that noise overnight, Sid?"

"Yep."

"What was it?"

"Well, Jen, it sounded like a cranky adult wombat. There is no adult in the Sanctuary so I don't know what it was. Let's check everything." They set off together down the paths between the cages.

"Sid, did you notice that a raven followed us from the time we found that baby wombat?"

"Yep. So what?"

"Dunno," said Jenny. "When we arrived back here, a raven flew into the tree by the animal hospital. As soon as we'd fixed the joey and put her in the cage with the other orphans, a raven flew onto the roof of the shelter and began to call. I think it was always the same bird. You could almost think it was speaking to the animal."

"Come on, now Jen, you can't believe that!"

"No I don't, but it was odd."

Sid and Jenny arrived at Wonder's cage. "Another oddity," muttered Sid. "Three young wagtails on the ground near the shelter." Jenny walked past the cage, looked down the side and whistled.

"Just look at this." She pointed to deep scratches in the wood made by Willit's claws. They followed his tracks along the soft dirt path. They found his tunnel under the wire fence. "What's going on Sid? "I don't know," he replied. "We'll find out tonight. We'll use the special video-camera and see what happens."

Late in the afternoon Jenny and Sid returned carrying a tripod with a camera on top. They focussed it on Willit's tunnel and Wonder's cage. They put a canvas sheet over the mouth of the tunnel. They left and the Sanctuary was silent.

Out in the bush Willit and his family slept until it was dark then they found some food. "Wee-leet-see-Won-der-now. Me-watch-black-track-road." When Flying Fox called they came immediately and watched their clever friend fly back and forth. He paused over Willit's head. "Go-go-go," he squeaked.

Lady and Thunder watched Willitt dash across to his tunnel and disappear. He hurtled out the other end, knocked the canvas cover off and stamped on it. In a few seconds he was looking over the fence at Wonder. "I'm going to dig you out," he called. "The ground on this side is soft. What's it like on your side?"
"It's hard, Papa. It's like a big sheet of smooth rock."
"Never mind, I'll break it." Willit began to dig. He had no trouble starting his tunnel outside the cage and he even got under the fence but when he tried to go up again, he had a problem with the big sheet of smooth rock.

He tunnelled this way and that. He looked for a crack or a break but there was none. He couldn't understand it. The stuff above his head was never ending. Willit had never seen concrete before.

He backed out into the air and stood up by the fence. Wonder had been listening to her Papa work under her feet. She didn't know how he could rescue her. Willit looked at her sad little face and thought hard.

"Don't worry," he said, "I'll do some bulldozing. Are there any breaks in this wooden fence?"

"Round here, Papa. Part of it opens when people come with food."

Willit trotted to the gate. He leant against the posts on either side. They were very firm. He stood on his hind legs and shook the gate, dropped to the ground, stepped back a bit and ran at it.

BANG!

Willit's head hit the heavy timber. He sat down with a thump. His whole body hurt. He looked at the gate. It was as tough and firm and strong as ever.

Inside the cage, Wonder hiccoughed. "Are you all right, Papa? You gave this horrid cage such a bang."

"I'm okay but I'm a bit dizzy." Willit leant against the gate. "I can't bulldoze this thing. I'm not sure what to do."

"Wee-leet-squeak-me."

Willit was cross and unhappy. "I can't squeak, but I can speak. What d'you want?" he growled.

"Mor-ning-here. You-make-noise. Pee-ple-come. You-go."

"You'll have to go, Papa. I'm okay. Come again at night time.

With a grunt of dismay, Willit ran to his tunnel. Flying Fox checked the road before the exhausted wombat stumbled across into the thick prickle bushes where Lady and Thunder waited. After a full night in the Sanctuary, Willit had achieved nothing. Sadly, they all walked deeper into the bush where they found Willit some food before huddling together in a temporary burrow under the strange skirts of a clump of grass trees. The wombats were soon fast asleep.

Inside the Sanctuary Jenny and Sid came to investigate. Sid walked all around the cage. "Look at this, Jenny. That adult wombat returned and dug several tunnels under the floor of the cage. Let's take the camera inside and watch the pictures."

They disappeared into the building, took the flash card out of the camera, popped it into the computer and sat back to watch the show.

"Good heavens," said Jenny. "Look at the size of that wombat. I've never seen such a big fellow. Look how he charged the gate. There's no doubt he wants that baby. What'll we do? If we knew where he was in the bush we could let the joey go but suppose the adult's gone? What then? It's a problem."

"Let's give it one more night," said Sid. "We'll put the cover back over the tunnel, leave the camera out and see if the big fellow returns."

Late that afternoon, Lady and Thunder left the shelter of the grass trees. Willit remained hidden.

One, Two and Three flew back and forth to the Sanctuary talking to Wonder and carrying messages to Lady and Thunder. They reported that Wonder's nose had healed and her foot no longer hurt.

Raven arrived and settled on the ground near Lady.

"Rark, rark, relay the news please," she asked.

"There's none," replied Lady.

"Something must be done. I'll see what I can think of." With her head on one side, Raven walked round and round in a circle till she got an idea. "What about Mrs Wallaby? She could jump into the cage, put Wonder in her pouch then jump out again."

"It wouldn't work," said Lady. "Mrs Wallaby couldn't go through the tunnel into the Sanctuary."

"Nor she could." Raven began to walk in circles again.

There was a loud rustling from the grass trees as Willit came lumbering out. "I know what to do," he said, "but I'll need both Lady and Thunder in the Sanctuary with me."

"What's your plan," asked Raven.

"I shall jump," he replied and he walked away.

Lady was astonished. She had no idea what Willit meant to do or what her job would be. It was time for a meal so she and Thunder followed Willit into the bush, leaving Raven walking in circles, wondering if a bird could ever understand a wombat!

One, Two and Three arrived back from the Sanctuary. "Where's Lady, Lady, Lady?" they all asked.

"Gone bush," said Raven. "Willit's got a plan that I don't understand. Can you lot stay awake after sunset?"

"Yes, Yes, Yes."

"Good. There's a full moon tonight. We'll perch in the tree over Wonder's cage. There's fun coming. Say nothing to Wonder but make sure that Flying Fox is here." Raven flew away.

The sun had gone and the moon was rising when the wombat family returned.
"Me-here. Me-rea-dy." Flying Fox was hanging around in a sheoak tree
"Thank you," said Willit. "Tonight I want Lady and Thunder to come with me, so please check the road carefully."
Flying Fox flew up and down. He relied mostly on hearing.
"Stand-still-stand-still" he called. A car rushed by. It was very frightening. Flying Fox checked the road again. Now it was safe. He swooped over the wombats squeaking "Go-go-go."

They didn't hesitate. Lady and Thunder had never trodden on a road before. The hard surface surprised them. They followed Willit straight through the tunnel and along the sandy path to the fence around Wonder's cage. Willit stood up against the fence. Lady did the same but she was unable to see across it. Wonder could smell Thunder and Lady. "Papa, Mumma, Thunder. You're all here!"
"Yes, and we're going to get you out," said Willit
"What will you do?"
"*I* will jump across this fence. *You* will climb on my back. *I* will stand up against the fence on your side. *You* will climb to the top of my head and that will bring *you* to the top of the fence. *You* will see Lady standing here in the path and *you* will jump onto her back. *Thunder* will help you down to the ground then *he* will lead you and Lady to safety through the tunnel."

"But where will you be when we go into the tunnel?" cried Lady, Thunder and Wonder.

"I'll stay in the cage and speak to Wonder's friends. I'll eat Wonder's food and drink her water. I'll jump out again. As I leave through the tunnel I'll fill it in. Those people will never know where Wonder went. We'll cross the black track together."

Up in the tree, Raven and the wagtails listened. None of them believed that Willit's plan would work.

"Stand well back, Wonder," called Willit.
The huge wombat backed away from the fence.
He took a short run then, using his back legs
like giant springs, launched himself into the air.
His head and shoulders went straight over the
fence but his tummy got stuck on the top rail.
He wriggled and kicked. Bit by bit he moved
forward until he half climbed, half fell over the
fence. Wonder rushed to him. They sniffed a
greeting. Willit dropped to the ground and
she scrambled onto his back. Once there
Wonder clung tightly as Willit used his front claws to help him
stand up against the fence.

40

"Goodbye, baby wombats," called Wonder. Turning her back to the cage she looked over the top of the fence and saw her dear Mumma and twin looking at her.

"Come on, my little Jumperoo," called Lady. "I'm ready for you." Wonder leapt straight onto her mother's back. Thunder stood by Lady's front legs and helped Wonder slide to the ground.

"Off you go," called Willit. "Wait for me at the edge of the black track."

With Thunder in front, a happy procession made its way to freedom.

Willit wandered over to the shelter where two wide-eyed wombats sat.

"Are you both quite happy?" he asked.

"Yes sir. People are kind and when we're old enough we think we'll be able to go back into the bush to live. Raven said that's what happened to Mrs Wallaby."

"That's true. Where will you go when you're free?"

"Wonder told us about your burrow near the pond. We thought we might visit you."

"What a good idea," said Willit. "Now I must go. *My* wombat family belongs in the bush."

Willit wandered over to the food bowls and ate some carrot and apple. He enjoyed these new flavours. He had a drink of water then approached the fence. Once again he used his strong back legs to propel himself upwards. This time he went straight over the top and onto the soft sand outside the cage. He lumbered to the tunnel, walked through it backwards so that he could break the walls then strolled out to join his cheering family and friends.

Willit dropped his head. "No fuss please. Flying Fox, is the road clear?"

Flying Fox sped up and down. "Go-go-go," he squeaked and the four wombats rushed across the road, through the prickly bushes and into an open space behind. Raven and the wagtails flew down onto the ground. Flying Fox hung around in a tree.

"Now where?" asked Raven.

"Back to the burrow by the pond," said Lady and Willit. "We'll start now."

While the birds flew to a tree to sleep and Flying Fox looked for a meal, Willit, Lady, Thunder and Wonder turned their noses in the direction of home.

They walked slowly that first night. Willit was very tired after his two great jumps. At dawn they found a cave, curled up close to one another and slept right through till sunset.

While the wombats slept, their friends spread the news of the great rescue. Raven, One, Two and Three, Flying Fox and Mrs Wallaby travelled all over the bush telling the story. Willie Wagtail left Wig-Wag sitting on her eggs and flew back to the Old Burrow to let everyone there know. Before long the bush was alive with the sound of voices talking about Willit the amazing wombat.

At the Sanctuary Sid and Jenny were stunned. They could hardly believe what had happened. Willit's cleverness in getting Wonder out and the part played by his mate and the other young wombat astonished them. They showed the video to everyone who worked in the Sanctuary. The story of the wombat that rescued its baby was told again and again. Without the film, no one would have believed it.

By the end of the second night Willit's family had reached the top of the rocky cliff near the pond. They paused to look down at their front door and were surprised to see many friends gathered on the sand. As they descended they heard voices calling,
"Welcome home. Welcome home. We've heard all about Wonder's adventure. We're glad you're back. We hope you don't go adventuring again."

The Great Wombat was there. He walked over to Willit, sniffed his ears then turned to the crowd. "You all know that Willit is special but did you know that Willit is my son? His mother called him Willit. I'm giving him another name. He is now Willit the Great Wombat. I'm too old for that job. It's his."

The bush rang with shouts of "Hooray."

Willit was surprised. He had never known for sure about his dad. It was good to hear the truth at last. "I don't think I'm ready to be a Great Wombat," he said, "but I'll try to be like my father. I'm not really special. I just love my family and all of you. I promise that Lady and I don't plan any more adventures. As for our twins – they must make up their own minds." He stopped talking for a minute and looked around. Then he said "I want to have a long talk to my dad, so good-morning everyone."

Led by Willit, who had found the last verse of his song, the wombats walked into the quiet comfort of the burrow by the pond for a long, well earned rest.

> Meeting any of us on a track,
> You shouldn't be surprised if we turn our backs.
> Just leave us alone when we run away,
> 'Cause we're really quite shy, in a wombatty way.

Willit's Song

Words and Melody: F Maber
Harmony: B Angus

1. I'm a wom - bat, I live in the bush, If
2. Strong and brave and I live un - der - ground, In
3. I've a tough plate hid - den in my rump, I
4. Meet - ing an - y of us on a track, You

some - thing's in my way, I give it a push. I'm like a bull - do - zer on
bur - row that I dig, with claws tough and round. I eat in the night and I
have - n't got much tail, just that bon - y lump and it is all cov - er'd with
should - n't be sur - prised if we turn our backs. Just leave us a - lone when we

four short legs and I onl - ly eat greens nev - er meat or eggs.
sleep by day then I vis - it my friends if I want to play.
skin so thick, that it keeps me quite safe from a bite or kick.

run a - way, 'cause we're real - ly qui - te shy, in a wom - bat - ty way!!

Lady's Lesson: How to tell a raven from a crow

A big black bird sat high in a tree
With very bright eyes it looked at me:
"Hello crow," I called to it
And its reply was "Cark "

A friend who heard said "That's no crow,
It's really a raven, didn't you know?"
"Hello raven," I called to the bird
And its reply was "Rark."

"If I call you crow you answer Cark,
If I call you raven you say Rark.
What are you then?" I asked that bird
As it hopped to a bough near me.

"I'm a raven I make a loud *Rark*,
You called me crow so I answered *Cark*.
But hackles on show and voice quite low
Argle-gargle's my call. I'm a Raven you know."

Acknowledgements:

More information about Northern Hairy-nosed Wombats can be found on the Wombat Foundation website: hhtp://www.wombatfoundation.com.au/index.html

Many people helped me as this story developed. Biological advice came from Dr Alan Horsup, Andrew Dinwoodie and others associated with Queensland Parks and Wildlife Service. Then there was an arachnologist at the Museum of WA, contacts in Gundaroo and Larissa Thies. Bruce Angus harmonised the little song. In addition there were several critical readers (one only 7 years old) who saw early versions of this story and asked questions that led me to reconsider parts of it. There were others who had input without knowing that I was listening!

To all of you and to Molly Angus, who did the pre-print edit and Alexander Hills who makes my characters beautiful, humorous and full of life, my sincere thanks. Last but not least, thank you to the staff at Pilpel Print for the quality and thoughtfulness of their work. There'd be no book without them!

Enquiries: Read Rebam Company, PO Box 725, South Perth. WA. 6951 or rrcompany@iinet.net.au

Printed and bound in Western Australia by Pilpel Print.

ISBN 978-0-646-49457-9

Bibliography:

The Secret Life of Wombats	James Woodford	Text Publishing 2002
The Wombat and the Dingo	I Smith & C Pugh	Sun Books 1984
Birdlife of Murdoch	Barbara D Porter (Ed)	Murdoch University 1985
Australian Native Plants	Wrigley & Fagg	Reed New Holland 2007 Concise Edition